Dear mouse friends,
Welcome to the world of

Geronimo Stilton

THE RODENT'S GAZETTE
EDITORIAL STAFF

 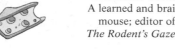 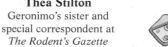

Geronimo Stilton
A learned and brainy
mouse; editor of
The Rodent's Gazette

Thea Stilton
Geronimo's sister and
special correspondent at
The Rodent's Gazette

   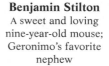

Trap Stilton
An awful joker;
Geronimo's cousin and
owner of the store
Cheap Junk for Less

Benjamin Stilton
A sweet and loving
nine-year-old mouse;
Geronimo's favorite
nephew

Geronimo Stilton

MOUSE OVERBOARD!

Scholastic Inc.

Copyright © 2014 by Edizioni Piemme S.p.A., Palazzo Mondadori, Via Mondadori 1, 20090 Segrate, Italy. International Rights © Atlantyca S.p.A. English translation © 2016 by Atlantyca S.p.A.

The publisher does not have any control over and does not assume any responsibility for author or third-party websites or their content.

GERONIMO STILTON names, characters, and related indicia are copyright, trademark, and exclusive license of Atlantyca S.p.A. All rights reserved. The moral right of the author has been asserted. Based on an original idea by Elisabetta Dami. www.geronimostilton.com

Published by Scholastic Inc., 557 Broadway, New York, NY 10012. SCHOLASTIC and associated logos are trademarks and/or registered trademarks of Scholastic Inc.

Stilton is the name of a famous English cheese. It is a registered trademark of the Stilton Cheese Makers' Association. For more information, go to www.stiltoncheese.com.

ISBN 978-0-545-87251-5

Text by Geronimo Stilton
Original title *Allarme... topo in mare!*
Cover by Francesco Castelli (design) and Christian Aliprandi (color)
Illustrations by Danilo Loizedda (design) and Christian Aliprandi (color)
Graphics by Chiara Cebraro

Special thanks to Anna Bloom
Translated by Lidia Morson Tramontozzi
Interior design by Kay Petronio

10 9 8 7 6 5 4 3 2 1   16 17 18 19 20

Printed in the U.S.A.   40

First printing 2016

A WHISKER SCORCHER

Holey **MELTED** cheese sticks, it was a hot day — a real WHISKER SCORCHER! The sun sizzled high over New Mouse City, and there wasn't a hint of a *breeze*. To make things worse, my **air conditioner** was on the blink.

Oof! It's so hot!

Broken MouseFreeze air conditioner

Oops, I almost forgot to introduce myself! My name is Stilton, *Geronimo Stilton*. I run *The Rodent's Gazette*, the most **famouse** daily newspaper on Mouse Island. Anyway, that day I was home catching up on my accounting. I was **head over whiskers** excited to see that my newspaper had also become the **BESTSELLING** paper on Mouse Island! Then the phone **rang**. At the other end, a familiar voice shrieked in my ear. **"Stilton!** You cheddarhead! I can't believe your newspaper has **outsold** mine! You better watch your tail! I will destroy *The Rodent's Gazette*!"

I will destroy The Rodent's Gazette!

Sally Ratmousen is the publisher of *The Daily Rat* and Geronimo's number one competitor.

It was Sally Ratmousen, editor of *The Daily Rat* — my nemesis! I wanted to tell her not to take my **success** so personally, but she had already hung up on me.

I tried to go back to my work, but I was **worried** about what Sally might do. And the heat was making fondue out of my brain!

In a panic, I called the repairmice at **MouseFreeze** Cooling Company. I had to get my **air conditioner** fixed! But the MouseFreeze receptionist had bad news.

"With this **heat wave**, all the repairmice are busy. You'll have to sit tight today!"

Sit tight?! I would **MELT** if I had to wait until **TOMORROW**. So I decided to get a little creative . . .

MouseFreeze offices!

HERE'S WHAT I DID TO TRY TO KEEP COOL . . .

FIRST TRY:

1 I made myself cheddar lemonade . . .

2 but it was too cold, and I got an awful STOMACHACHE!

SECOND TRY:

1 I took an ICE BATH . . .

2 but I had to get out quickly because I was turning into a MOUSICLE!

THIRD TRY:

1 I tied ICE POPS on my ears and under my paws . . .

2 but my fur got all STICKY and attracted fruit flies!

FOURTH TRY:

1 I decided to take a cold shower . . .

2 but I SLIPPED and ended up inside Hannibal's fishbowl!

After all of that, I finally remembered that I still had an old **FAN** in the attic. It was my last hope for staying cool!

But . . . where had I put the key? Was it **HANGING** in the hall? Did I put it in my desk drawer? Was it in the kitchen? Or had I **HIDDEN** it inside a vase in the living room?

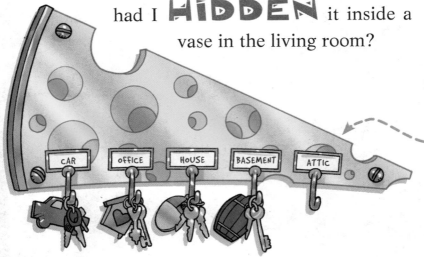

I looked everywhere until I **finally** found it — still inside the attic door's keyhole! I went in and started to look for the fan. But I quickly got distracted. The attic was full of mementos from my many ADVENTURES. I spotted the COWBOY hat the Red Bandit had given to me, and the uniform I had worn when I won the Karate World Championship!

SO MANY MARVEMOUSE MEMORIES!

That's where the key is!

My Attic

1) The golf clubs I used when I won the Super Mouse Cup with Grandfather William.
2) The wet suit I wore while scuba diving off Shell Island.
3) The old suitcase I used while vacationing at the Ratty Tatty Hotel.
4) The skis I used while skiing on Frozen Fur Peak.
5) The basketball signed by Bounce Ballmouse.
6) The soccer cleats I wore when I won the Mouse Island soccer tournament.
7) The cowboy hat the Red Bandit gave me.

8) The chef's hat I wore during the Super Chef Contest.

9) The uniform I wore during the Karate World Championship.

10) My favorite furry snow boots.

11) The astronaut suit I wore during my space mission.

12) The crystal gondola Petunia Pretty Paws bought me, which led to my adventure in Venice.

13) My great-grandmother Ratricia's collection of chamber pots.

14) The fan Thea gave me.

ACHOO! ACHOO!
ACHOO! ACHOO!

With a start, I remembered the whole **reason** I had come to the attic — the fan! There it was high up on a far shelf, right above my great-grandmother's **chamber pot** collection!

The chamber pots were all colors, shapes, and sizes. Some had **designs** of different kinds of cheeses; some were made of **CRYSTAL**; some were shaped like Greek

columns; others were hand-painted. There was even one in the **shape** of a cat's head . . .

I reached out my **PAW** to get the fan and disturbed a huge cloud of dust.

I sneezed so much, I lost my balance and crashed to the floor.

I disturbed a cloud of dust and began to sneeze. Achoo!

I lost my balance and crashed to the floor!

Everything on the shelves fell on me . . .

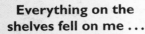

. . . including an extremely heavy chamber pot!

What a headache!

Even worse, I ended up pulling everything on the shelves down with me, including the chamber pots!

CRASH! BANG! SMASH! BANG! BOOM!

With a final **CRASH**, the massive chamber pot shaped like a cat's head fell right on top of me. Cheese niblets! That made me see a billion stars — and all their planets!

What a headache!

Rubbing my head, I took the fan down to the living room. Then I sat on my favorite pawchair with an ice pack on my head and the fan blowing at full speed.

AHH, WHat a PeLieF! I was finally comfortable.

I had almost dozed off when the doorbell rang, jolting me awake.

DING-DONG! DIIIIING-DONG! DING-DOOOOONG!

Who could it be? Curious, I hightailed it to open the door.

Ahh, much better!

GRAAAANDSON!

As soon as I opened the door, I was OVERWHELMED by a booming yell.

"GRAAAANDSON!"

Huh???

Moldy mozzarella! It was my grandfather William Shortpaws! I didn't have a chance to ask why he was here, because he immediately roared, "GRANDSON! What are you doing cooped up in the house with the shades down? Snoring away the afternoon in your pawchair, I'll bet!"

"Actually, with this HEAT WAVE, I can't seem to concentrate. And my AIR CONDITIONER is broken, so —" I tried to explain, but Grandfather interrupted.

"I don't want to hear any excuses! Since it seems like you have NOTHING to do here, you won't mind that I'm sending you to Portugal! A friend of mine needs a favor, and you're the best mouse for the job."

"Me? Go to PORTUGAL? When? How? And, most important, why?"

"No questions!" my grandfather snapped.

"Hop in the van and get going!"

Only then did I notice there was a **MINIVAN** parked in front of my house.

The van was overloaded with every kind of **LUGGAGE**. There was even a huge inflatable duck float!

My sister, Thea; my cousin Trap; my nephew Benjamin; and his friend Bugsy Wugsy were all ready and waiting for me.

You look stressed!

Argh!

Uncle G, come with us!

Um . . .

"Are you all going to **PORTUGAL** with me?" I asked.

"You bet we are, Cuz!" Trap said.

"I can't go to Portugal now!" I protested. "I'm very **BUSY** with *The Rodent's Gazette*!" I wanted to **STICK** around and see what kind of revenge Sally Ratmousen might be plotting.

"**No excuses, Grandson!**" my **GRANDFATHER** thundered. "I'll take care of the newspaper for you while you're gone."

"You seem a little down," Thea said. "You have bags under your eyes, and your fur is faded. You're too stressed! You have to come with us. It'll be good for you!"

I was about to refuse, but Bugsy took my right PAW, and Benjamin took my left one. They LOOKED up at me with big, wide eyes.

"Come with us to PORTUGAL! We'll have a blast!" they said.

Hooray!

Everyone to Portugal!

Off we go!

How could I refuse them? "Oh, all right. But I have to PACK and —"

I didn't even have time to finish my sentence before everybody pushed me into the van, shouting, "Yaaaay! We're off to Portugal!"

I looked out the window to say good-bye to Grandfather and saw Aunt Sweetfur and Uncle Grayfur. Aunt Sweetfur looked worried as she waved her handkerchief at me. She dried a tear and called, "Take care, my little nephew."

She always worries when we go on trips. But this time, she seemed more anxious than usual! Uncle Grayfur waved good-bye. "Once you're on board, make us PROUD, Nephew!"

How Strange!

Why was Aunt Sweetfur so worried about me this time? **Why** did Uncle Grayfur tell me to make them proud "on board"? **Why** did Grandfather need me to help someone in Portugal?

"What are we doing in Portugal?" I asked suspiciously.

Thea smiled at me. "We've all been officially invited to Lisbon, PORTUGAL, for a very important historic commemoration," she said. "It turns out that we Stiltons are the descendants of a *famouse* Portuguese rodent!"

Hee, hee!

Then she **glanced** at **TRAP**, and he chuckled to himself.

"What exactly will I be doing at this **historic** commemoration? Who is the friend of Grandfather's who needs a favor?" I asked.

"I don't want to say too much and **SPOIL** the surprise," Thea said. "But you'll be doing what our ancestor became famouse for."

Thea and Trap exchanged a look. Trap chuckled again.

Why *all the mystery?* I wondered.

I didn't have much time to think more about it, because Bugsy Wugsy **shouted** in my ear, "Uncle G! We're at the airport! Lisbon is waiting for us!"

Thea checked her watch. "CHEESE AND CRACKERS! We're late! We have to *hurry*, or we'll miss our flight!"

I trudged into the airport LOADED down with the luggage. I wondered who our Portuguese ancestor would turn out to be. Was it a famous writer? Or a SCIENTIST?

Argh!

Or maybe an **inventor**?

I kept thinking about it the whole time we were waiting for our *PLANE* and while we were boarding. I was so immersed in my thoughts that I tripped over my own **Paws** and sprawled in the aisle! Luggage flew in all directions, and the *inflatable duck float* wound up around an old rodent's neck!

All the passengers burst out **LAUGHING**.

"Ha, ha, ha!"

"Hey, isn't that Geronimo Stilton?"

"I didn't know he was such a **klutz**!"

"How embarrassing for him!"

Squeeeeak! Poor me!

The old rodent with the enormouse *inflatable duck* around her neck frowned at me.

"You should be more careful!" she scolded.

My fur turned pink with embarrassment. I picked up all the luggage and mumbled my apologies. I finally got to my seat and sank **DEEPLY** into it. To take my mind off things, I picked up the travel guide on Portugal and began to read it.

Hmm . . . interesting!

Destination: Portugal

WHERE IS IT?

Portugal is the westernmost country in mainland Europe. It borders Spain on the north and east, and it stretches into the Atlantic Ocean on the south and west. Portugal has over eleven hundred miles of coastline.

WHAT'S THE WEATHER LIKE?

Portugal's climate varies depending on the region. It is commonly hotter and drier in the south, where Lisbon is located, and cooler and wetter in the north. The weather is warmest from June through mid-September, which makes summer a nice time to visit.

DON'T LEAVE HOME WITHOUT . . .

- A pocket dictionary
- Sunscreen
- An umbrella

Portugal and Navigation

At the beginning of the fifteenth century, Henry the Navigator, son of the king of Portugal, organized many sea expeditions. He hoped to establish new colonies in West Africa and take advantage of the resources found there — particularly slaves, gold, and sugar.

In 1497, Portuguese navigator VASCO DA GAMA led the first European expedition to reach southern India by sea.

Da Gama left Lisbon on July 8, 1497, on his flagship, SÃO GABRIEL, and was accompanied by three other ships: the SÃO RAFAEL, the BERRIO, and a smaller vessel that carried supplies.

In November, he sailed around the CAPE OF GOOD HOPE (which had previously been reached by Bartolomeu Dias, another Portuguese explorer). On May 20, 1498, he landed on the southwestern coast of India. It was the first time a European ship had ever been there!

THE GREAT
VASCO DA GAMA

While reading the **GUIDEBOOK**, I kept wondering who our famous Portuguese ancestor could be. Did we look alike? He was probably a mouse who loved books and had a fear of traveling like me. Maybe he even got **seasick** just like I do!

I **TAPPED** Thea on the shoulder. "Did our famous ancestor look like me? I bet we have a lot in common."

She burst out **laughing**. "Not at all! He was bold, courageous, and not afraid of anything."

I tried not to look offended. "So who is it? I have to know!"

Trap chuckled. "Tell him," he said. "He can't escape now, unless, of course, he jumps out of the plane!"

Thea smiled. "Well, okay. Our famouse ancestor is . . . *the great explorer Vasco da Gama!*"

My whiskers trembled. "The great Portuguese Navigator?" I shrieked.

Benjamin, who had overheard our conversation, started squeaking with excitement. "Yeah, that's the one! Isn't that fabumouse?"

"I don't understand," I muttered, perplexed. "Are you a thousand percent sure

Ack!

that we are Vasco da Gama's descendants? We don't look anything like him!"

Trap pinched my ear playfully. "You're so wrong, Cuz. You look a lot like him. Both of you have two ears! Both of you have a tail and whiskers! You're practically identical! *A real slice off the old cheese block!*"

"That's not true!" I retorted. "I'm the opposite of Vasco da Gama in every way!"

"All of us *Stiltons* are his descendants," Thea explained. "They just found out! That's why we are invited on this fabumouse reenactment of his first expedition. All the descendants of those who participated in that landmark voyage will be on the cruise. Isn't it mousefastic?" Thea looked thrilled.

I became paler than a ball of FRESH mozzarella.

He was fearless!

I hate to travel!

He discovered a new route to India!

I sometimes have trouble finding my way home!

He was always ready for adventure!

I'm a big 'fraidy mouse!

"Did you say *cruise*? You mean we'll be traveling by S-S-Sea?" I asked.

"Yes! Isn't it wild? We'll be on an old sailing ship, just like the one VASCO DA GAMA used!" squeaked Bugsy Wugsy, full of excitement.

Thea handed me an ivory-colored envelope. "This is the *official invitation.* You'll be the guest of honor."

I opened the envelope with trembling paws and read the letter.

Holey cheese! There it was. The letter said that I, *Geronimo Stilton*, was not only one of Vasco da Gama's descendants but that I had to take on his role in the reenactment!

"NO WAY!" I cried in exasperation. "I get SEASICK. Besides, I don't even know how to steer a ROWBOAT, so how am I supposed to play Vasco da Gama?

The Vasco da Gama Anniversary Cruise

DEAR MR. STILTON,

WE ARE HONORED TO INFORM YOU THAT AS A DESCENDANT OF THE GREAT PORTUGUESE NAVIGATOR VASCO DA GAMA, YOU AND YOUR FAMILY ARE OFFICIALLY INVITED TO RETRACE THE PRINCIPAL STEPS OF HIS VOYAGE TO INDIA ON BOARD THE *SÃO GABRIEL*, AN EXACT REPLICA OF THE SHIP USED BY VASCO DA GAMA.

YOU WILL HAVE THE HONOR OF TAKING THE ROLE OF THE GREAT NAVIGATOR AND STEERING THE SHIP YOURSELF. AS HIS DESCENDANT, YOU WILL CERTAINLY UNDERSTAND ALL THERE IS TO KNOW ABOUT NAVIGATION!

WE WILL EAGERLY AWAIT YOU IN LISBON ON PIER 7 ON JULY 7.

BEST WISHES,

Julio Rattio

SECRETARY OF STATE FOR TOURISM

I'm seasick!

Your brain must have as many holes as a slice of Swiss if you think I'm going to board an ancient ship and run the risk of being shipwrecked! As soon as we land, I'm getting on the next flight home!"

Trap pinched my ear again. "Not possible, Cuz! You can't go back. But don't worry. I brought this inflatable duck in case we get shipwrecked."

"Look, Geronimo, I'm sorry, but you can't refuse," Thea said FIRMLY. She leaned in close. "The tourism secretary is an old friend of Grandfather's," she whispered.

"Secretary Rattio thinks there's someone signed up for the **REENACTMENT** who isn't who they say they are."

"What's that have to do with me?" I whispered back.

"Grandfather and the secretary want you to **unmask** the potential saboteur!"

Moldy mozzarella! I was stuck!

A Slice off the Old Cheese Block

We finally landed in Lisbon. As soon as we **got off** the plane, a waiting band struck up the national anthem of Mouse Island.

We all placed our right **paws** over our hearts and sang the anthem together. What a fabumouse welcome!

A thousand tails . . .

A thousand tails . . .

A thousand tails . . .

"*A thousand voices squeak as one.*
A thousand tails proudly wag.
A thousand whiskers boldly quiver.
A thousand paws raise your yellow flag!
Under our fur,
a thousand hearts beat for you,
sweet, sweet Mouse Island."

Despite my worries about the coming sea voyage, my whiskers trembled with joy at hearing the **Mouse Island anthem!** We walked toward the secretary for tourism on the **loooong** red carpet rolled out for us. Trap **pinched** my ear.

"Cousin, I'm warning you. For once, try not to **embarrass** us —"

But Trap didn't have time to finish his sentence. I was so excited to meet the secretary for tourism, I **TRIPPED** on the edge of the carpet. **1** Then I frantically **GRASPED** the air in an attempt to keep my balance, but, despite my arm **FLAPPING**, I fell smack on my head! **2** (Luckily, the carpet was soft!) From there, I tumbled into a mousetacular **somersault** . . . **3** and found myself back on my paws in front of the secretary! **4**

MY ARRIVAL IN LISBON!

1) I was so excited, I tripped on the edge of the rug!

2) I tried to keep my balance, but I fell on my head!

3) I performed a mouse-tacular somersault . . .

4) . . . and found myself in front of the secretary!

The secretary applauded with GUSTO. "Welcome to Portugal, Mr. Stilton! We see immediately that you are a bold, athletic, and courageous rodent — just like your ancestor Vasco da Gama! You are the spitting image of him — you're a real slice off the old cheese block!"

I blushed pink from the tip of my tail to the tips of my ears. "Um . . . thank you . . .

but I don't really think I'm **anything** like Vasco da Gama . . ."

Everybody burst out laughing.

No one laughed harder than the secretary. "Ha, ha, ha! So humble, Mr. Stilton! Just like Vasco da Gama! Like I said, a real slice off the old cheese block."

Trap stepped in before I could say anything else. "You have to excuse my cousin, Mr. Secretary. He's a very MODEST mouse. Everyone can clearly see that he and our ancestor have a lot in common. They both have two ears, two eyes, and one tail!"

I gave up! There was nothing I could do. Everyone was convinced I was just like Vasco da Gama! I didn't have time to think anymore about it. The secretary invited us to get in a CAR that was waiting for us at the end of the runway. I shook Secretary Rattio's paw and thanked him for his welcome. I was about to get in when he tapped me on my shoulder.

"Mr. Stilton, I know that besides being Vasco da Gama's DESCENDANT, you're also an extremely competent DETECTIVE. Your grandfather speaks highly of you. As he may have mentioned, I suspect that someone is planning to sabotage the *São Gabriel* voyage! Please find out who it is. You're the only one who can help me!"

As much as I was dreading getting on that boat, I could see the secretary was very worried. He had been so welcoming — I wanted to HELP him if I could. "You can count on this mouse," I said.

The secretary looked relieved. "The ship will launch tomorrow at dawn," he said. "In the meantime, you can SEE a little of our **BEAUTIFUL** city. Bernardo Almouse, your driver, will be your guide and also your bodyguard. Thank you, Mr. Stilton — and keep your **EYES OPEN**. Portugal's **honor** is in your paws!"

THIS IS WHAT
I CALL MUSIC!

As soon as we got in the car, Bernardo Almouse hit the gas, and we took off. The tires screeched like a scared cat. Then he turned the radio on at full blast. He sighed happily. "This is what I call **MUSIC**! This is fado. It's traditional Portuguese music."

Lulled by the melancholy melodies, I forgot all my worries and became immersed in the beautiful sights of the city as they flashed by.

"Are you ready to **DISCOVER** Lisbon?" Bernardo Almouse shouted.

Fado

Fado is a famous genre of Portuguese music that became popular in the 1820s and '30s. It was commonly performed in taverns and cafés. The word *fado* means "fate" in Portuguese. This type of music is often emotional and deals with heartfelt stories of everyday life.

BERNARDO ALMOUSE

A mouse of many resources!

He's not just a CHAUFFEUR. He's also a TOUR GUIDE, a BODYGUARD, and a COOK. He specializes in traditional Portuguese dishes made with dried cod. Bernardo is also an extremely talented SAILOR. He has traveled the seven seas and knows thousands of mysterious legends about the ocean.

He is not AFRAID of anything or anyone. He's always ready with a joke and is a big talker.

Bernardo's real PASSION is fado. He listens to it continuously on his car stereo. He even plays the Portuguese guitar and sings fado regularly.

He's secretly IN LOVE with the beautiful Maria do Sol, the glamorous and very famous fado singer.

He has fifteen cousins, all of whom are CHEFS.

LISBON: Lisbon is the capital city of Portugal. The city has a great deal of charm and history. Narrow, steep streets run through its heart. Lisbon lies on the Tagus River and sits on the slopes of several hills. Because of this, there are many breathtaking scenic overlooks.

"You're going to love it! We'll visit the Grand Oceanarium, the National Park, and Jerónimos Monastery, and we'll end at the Belém Tower!"

"What an **amazing** itinerary!" Thea exclaimed.

"AWESOME!" Benjamin squeaked. "The Oceanarium is one of the biggest aquariums in the world!"

"Bernardo, you didn't mention the most important thing," I said.

"What did I forget?" he asked.

"You forgot **lunch**! And a snack! And **dinner**!" I exclaimed.

Bernardo happily twirled his whiskers.

"*Nenhum problema*!* I have that planned, too! We'll have a picnic lunch at the **PARK OF NATIONS** prepared by my cousin Codmouse the First. Then we'll stop for

* *Nenhum problema* means "no problem" in Portuguese.

a snack at the most famouse bakery in Lisbon, where my cousin Codmouse the Second works, and have dinner at Casa de Fado, where my cousin Codmouse the Third works. Then we'll spend the night at the **HOTEL** my cousin Codmouse the Fourth owns."

A picnic at the Park of Nations!

"How many COUSINS do you have?" Trap asked, laughing.

A snack at a famouse bakery!

"Fifteen! And they're all chefs like my great-uncle, the cook who prepared the BEST BACALHAU — salted cod — in all of Lisbon! But enough talking. Here's the OCEANARIUM! Everybody out. The tour starts now!"

Then bedtime at the hotel!

BENJAMIN AND BUGSY WUGSY'S NOTES

THE LISBON OCEANARIUM

Opened in 1998, the Oceanarium is a large aquarium dedicated to marine species that live in the oceans, and to their habitats.

Here we are at the entrance of the Oceanarium. It's truly amazing, mouselets! Uncle Trap was a prankster. (As usual!)

The Oceanarium is home to hundreds of different species of plants and animals. It has over one million visitors each year!

The shark tank was incredible. Too bad Uncle G fainted from fright! (As usual!)

The Park of Nations was the site of the 1998 Lisbon World Exposition, a world's fair that marked the five hundredth anniversary of Vasco da Gama's famous expedition. Inside the park, there are shops, restaurants, gardens, and a train station.

The Jerónimos Monastery is located in the Belém district of Lisbon. It was built by King Manuel I. Many explorers, including Vasco da Gama, stopped here to pray before leaving on expeditions.

Near the monastery is a bakery called Pastéis de Belém, where the specialty is custard tarts, a classic Portuguese treat.

Here's a *casa de fado*, where popular Portuguese music is played.

Welcome Aboard!

I couldn't enjoy the tour of the city as much as everyone else. The next morning we'd be sailing on a rickety old ship. Shiver my whiskers! Would we end up stranded on a desert island? Would we end up as a **snack** for sharks? I almost fainted from fright when I saw them in the Oceanarium! And to top it all off, someone apparently wanted to SABOTAGE our voyage!

The secretary's words kept popping into my head: "Keep your eyes open . . ."

Keep my **EYES OPEN** I did! I was so stressed, I couldn't close my eyes the entire night! *Squeak!*

The following morning, when Bernardo Almouse took us to the Lisbon port to board

the ship, I had **bags** under both eyes, my
whiskers were trembling
with stress, and my
eyelids kept falling
shut. I was even
snoring while
standing up!
*"Zzzz!
Zzzz!"*

Zzzz!
Zzzz!

Are you
sleeping?

The secretary
stared at me, confused.

"Are you sleeping? I had asked you to
keep your **EYES OPEN** . . ."

Always alert, Thea quickly **ELBOWED**
me in the ribs. "Don't worry, Mr. Secretary.
My brother is completely awake . . . In
fact, I've never seen him more bright-eyed
and bushy-tailed!"

I tried to open my eyes wider. "Yes, yes,

I'm very awake. Look, Secretary Rattio, my **EYES** are open and ready to spot a saboteur!"

The secretary slapped me so hard on my back that I *STAGGERED* forward.

"That's what I like to see, Mr. Stilton. You're awake, brave, and ready for anything, just like your ancestor **VASCO DA GAMA**! Hurry now, put on the costume. The ship is about to set sail!"

A few minutes later, we were on board the São Gabriel, a replica of Vasco da Gama's famous flagship.

The ship's entire crew, **dressed** in period clothes like us, was lined up on the deck of the *São Gabriel*. We all looked like we had stepped right out of history! Everyone stared at me in complete silence. You could have heard a cheese slice *drop*. It seemed like

the crew was expecting something important to happen — but what?

I stared back at them, my fur turning **PINK** with embarrassment, not sure what to do.

"Why are they all staring at me?" I whispered to Thea. "Do I have a pimple on my snout? Do I have cheese crumbs in my whiskers?"

I was stumped. **Fortunately**, right at that moment, I felt someone tap me on my shoulder. I turned and saw a **big mustache**

Why are you all staring at me?

attached to a familiar smiling face . . . It was Bernardo Almouse!

"Mr. Stilton," he whispered. "I mean, Admiral! You have to address the crew to start the voyage off on the right paw!"

He handed me a **sheet** of paper with some pointers for my speech. "It's lucky for you I'm also going on this voyage. Who knows what kind of trouble you might get into without me!"

"What are you doing here?" I whispered.

He winked at me. "Didn't you know? I'm also a descendant of someone who participated in Vasco da Gama's expedition. I'm the helmsmouse's great-great-great-great-grandson! The secretary also wanted me to help you track down the potential troublemaker. Better get going with that speech. The crew is getting impatient!"

Trap pinched me on the ear. "Say something, Geronimo. Don't be a scaredy-mouse!"

Thea patted my back. "Hurry up and give your speech, Geronimo. The crew is starting to get cranky."

"You can do it, Uncle," Benjamin exclaimed. "You're representing all of us!"

I quickly looked at the notes Bernardo had handed me. I cleared my throat, stood up straight, squared my shoulders, and tried to look as confident as possible, just like a REAL ADMIRAL would. I gazed out at the crowd. I wondered which mouse out there might be up to no good . . .

"Dear rodent friends, welcome aboard the *São Gabriel*! We've all been granted

Dear rodent friends . . .

the tremendmouse honor of reliving the experience of **VASCO DA GAMA'S** first expedition! I hope everyone will do his or her best for the success of this voyage. And now, all mice to their places! Raise the anchor! *Set sail!*"

I turned to Benjamin. "How did I do?" I asked.

"You were awesome, Uncle G!" he answered.

"Three cheers for Geronimo Stilton, our captain!" the crew exclaimed.

Within a few minutes, the ship was headed toward the open sea. The water shimmered in the early morning light, and the deck was busy with crewmice.

THE SHIPS USED BY VASCO DA GAMA

Vasco da Gama took four ships on his expedition: the flagship *São Gabriel*, where he was in command; the *São Rafael*; the *Berrio*; and another, smaller ship that carried supplies. The crew consisted of about 170 men across all four ships.

Mouse Overboard!

As soon as we got to the open sea, Bernardo took me to my cabin. He handed me a nautical chart that was exactly like the one used by the great Vasco Da Gama.

"Admiral, what's our route? A real captain always knows the best way!"

I squinted at the chart, not sure what I was looking at. I turned it one way and then the other. I flipped it over and then back again.

Rancid ricotta! I couldn't understand one bit of it! Bernardo winked at me.

Which way do I read it?

???

VASCO DA GAMA'S ROUTE

Vasco da Gama left Lisbon on July 8, 1497, passed by the Canary Islands, and continued along the coast of Africa to the island of Santiago, Cape Verde. After sailing for several months, he went around the Cape of Good Hope and crossed the Indian Ocean. He landed in southern India on May 20, 1498.

"A **real captain** knows seas and currents, sails and ropes, anchors and helms!" he said. "But, between the two of us mice, I think you're a **landlubber** and you don't understand any of it!"

"I never said I was a good sailor," I answered, a little offended. "Everybody knows I don't know how to sail, and I get **seasick**!"

Bernardo burst out laughing. "Don't worry! I'll help you get up to speed," he said. "A **real captain** also knows every single mouse in his crew. Why don't you start by getting to know them? That will give you a chance to see if any of them seem **SUSPICIOUS**. I'll take care of the navigating!"

Bernardo handed me a folder with the names and roles of every crew member. I rounded up Benjamin and Bugsy Wugsy.

With them at my side, I **STAGGERED** toward the bridge in an attempt to get to know my crew.

But, unfortunately, the ship was swaying side to side. My stomach did flip-flops, and my snout got warm.

Waves of nausea **rolled** over me as the ocean waves rolled past the ship. But even though I was getting seasick, I decided to keep going. I didn't want to be **EMBARRASSED** in front of my crew. And besides, I needed to keep my eyes open for anyone who might want to sabotage our voyage.

Sāo Gabriel's Crew

GERONIMO STILTON
Admiral

BERNARDO ALMOUSE
Helmsmouse

GEORGE GORGONZOLA
First Officer

MATTHEW MAYO
Onboard Doctor

PETER TAILWIND
Sailor

BRAN ZINO
Sailor

MARIO MALGA
Sailor

PAULO SAILMOUSE
Cabin Mouse

BENJAMIN STILTON
Student Sailor

BUGSY WUGSY
Student Sailor

TRAP STILTON
Onboard Cook

THEA STILTON
Helmsmouse Helper

MY SEASICKNESS GOT WORSE ...

I LOOKED OVER THE SIDE ...

AND SOMEONE SHOVED ME!

Unfortunately, just as I was about to squeak to George Gorgonzola, my **SEASICKNESS** got even worse. **①**

To hide how awful I felt, I **LOOKED OVER** the side of the ship to admire the scenery, my fur turning greener than a **moldy** cheese rind. **②**

"Ah, what a beautiful sea! It's so blue!"

SUDDENLY, I felt two paws on my shoulders. Before I could *turn* around, someone **SHOVED**

me overboard! I landed in the water with a giant **SPLASH**! **3**

FORTUNATELY, Benjamin saw what happened. He shouted for help, and an alarm resonated throughout the ship:

"MOUSE OVERBOARD!"

Someone threw me a life preserver . . . but it landed smack on my head!

"SQUEAAAK! OUCH!"

Ouuuuch!

FISHY FIRST AID

The crew fished me out of the water and rushed me to the infirmary. Dr. Matthew Mayo was waiting for me. He treated the **ENORMOUSE LUMP** on my head with a compress made of **FR°ZEN C°D**.

"Be sure to keep the fish on your injury!" Dr. Mayo said. "It **smells** a little, but it'll do wonders!"

Ouch!

Yuck!

In fact, it didn't just smell. It really, really stunk!

As soon as the doctor left the infirmary, Thea, Trap, Benjamin, and Bugsy Wugsy came to see me. They all looked very worried.

"I think someone **pushed me**!" I said.

"Something **strange** happened to me, too," Trap said. "While I was cooking the **fish** for tonight's dinner, someone moved around the food on the **STOVE** a second before it would have burned! **WHO** would've done that?"

"That's **weird**!" Bugsy Wugsy added. "Earlier today,

I tried and tried to fold the **sails**, but I couldn't do it. When I came back later, **someone** had secretly folded them for me!"

Benjamin nodded. "The same thing happened to me. I tried to wind the **ropes**, but I made a mess of them and got all tangled up. When I went back later to fix them, they were all neatly coiled. Maybe there's a **ghost on board**!"

"There's no ghost," I said, shaking my head. "But Secretary Rattio did warn me to keep my **EYE** out for a mouse who might be trying to sabotage the voyage."

Thea shook her head. "But the mysterious rodent Benjamin, Bugsy Wugsy, and Trap described was being HELPFUL. A real saboteur would want to cause as much *trouble* as possible. I think we're dealing with **TWO DIFFERENT RODENTS!**"

"Well, whoever shoved me in the water wasn't being **HELPFUL!**" I said, massaging my aching snout. "You might be right. We have to try to catch the saboteur with his paws in the cookie jar!"

"While you rest, I'm going to go with Trap to check out the kitchen," Thea said. "Maybe I'll find a **CLUE** there."

Once everyone left, I fell asleep with the frozen codfish compress on my head. I woke up several hours later surrounded by **FLIES!** The frozen cod had melted, and it was even **smellier** than before! I quickly washed off and went up on the ship's deck to investigate . . . and a **HUGE** seagull swooped down and started to peck me!

I smelled so much like a **fish** that the seagull thought I was one! Desperate to get away, I jumped into a nearby lifeboat and **hid** under the tarp. The seagull soon flew away. **PHEW!** But just as I was about to crawl back out, the lifeboat *plummeted* down into the water!

Oh no! I would never **SURVIVE** alone

Ouch!
Go away!

in a lifeboat! Luckily, I could hear Bernardo Almouse calling for help.

"**MOUSE OVERBOARD!**" he yelled.

Once they had fished me out of the sea for the second time, Bernardo pulled me aside. "This was no accident, Admiral Stilton. **Someone** cut the rope securing the lifeboat!"

Someone was definitely up to **no good** — and it seemed like they were determined to ruin the voyage by sending me to the bottom of the **OCEAN**!

THE SABOTEUR!

My whiskers trembled with stress. "It was the saboteur! I'm not safe anywhere!"

"Don't worry, Admiral. I saw everything!" BERNARDO grabbed the first officer by the tail. "Here's the saboteur! It's George Gorgonzola!"

A second later, Thea and Trap came from the KITCHEN holding the cabin mouse by the arms.

He won't strike again!

Ah!

It's Paulo, the cabin mouse!

We caught him!

"Here is the saboteur! It's Paulo, the cabin mouse!" Thea shouted.

"Everybody, stop!" I exclaimed. "We have one too many saboteurs here! **Bring** them to my cabin. I'll get to the bottom of this!"

BERNARDO took them by the ears and dragged them to my cabin.

"Which one of you is the saboteur?" I asked.

Paulo the cabin mouse burst into tears. To our surprise, he reached up and took off his hair! Then he pulled off a mask! He was a she!

"I'm not a **SABOTEUR**!" she said through her tears. "I did crash the reenactment, but I'd never want to ruin it."

I handed her my handkerchief. She dried her **TEARS** and continued. "My name is Paulina Pecorina, and I really wanted to be part of this voyage. My great-great-great-great-grandfather was Vasco da Gama's personal chef, but his name was never included on the

Sob!

The Transformation of Paulo Sailmouse

BEFORE   AFTER

crew list. I didn't get an official reenactment invitation, so I boarded under a false name and COOKED in secret!"

"That's why Trap's been serving such delicious dishes! It's been you the WHOLE TIME!" Thea exclaimed. "You even kept Trap's fish from burning."

"Give me a little credit!" Trap Muttered.

Paulina blushed. "I just love cooking. I'm sorry about all this — but I never sabotaged anyone. You have to BELIEVE me!"

"I do believe you," I reassured her. "In fact, from now on you'll be the official SHIP COOK!" I said. "I'll let Secretary Rattio know about the error and have him add you to the official VOYAGE participant list."

Paulina dried her tears. "Thank you, Admiral Stilton! That's very generous. I'm going to cook all my great-great-great-great-

The Story of Paulina Pecorina, Aspiring Chef

Paulina's great-great-great-great-grandfather was Vasco da Gama's personal chef.

But he was never identified in the ship's records, so Paulina joined the reenactment in secret!

Paulina cooked when no one was watching . . .

. . . until she got caught!

grandfather's secret recipes. They're all here in this old recipe book I brought. It's been handed down in my family for generations!"

"That recipe book has to be worth its weight in **GOLD**!" Trap exclaimed. "We could publish it and become millionaires!"

"Paws down, Trap!" we all *SHOUTED* together. "The **RECIPE** book is **SECRET**!"

With one potential saboteur cleared, we had one suspect left. I turned to the first officer, George Gorgonzola. Suddenly, he took off his *hat*, *tore* off his false WHiSKeRS, and removed his mask! What an **ENORMOUSE** surprise! It was none other than

My secret recipe book!

Wow!

my **NEMESIS, SALLY RATMOUSEN**!

"It's me, *Stilton*!" Sally snarled. "When I came to your house to continue our conversation, I overheard that you had been invited to **PORTUGAL**. I followed you here and snuck on board this ship under a **false name**! I wanted to show everyone what a fool you really are!" Sally explained triumphantly. "I took photos of all your most embarrassing

THE TRANSFORMATION OF GEORGE GORGONZOLA

BEFORE

AFTER

moments! I'm going to do a front-page story all about how ridiculous you are. It will sell out — *mark my words*! I can just see the headline:

> ## Newsmouse Disgraces Famouse Navigator! Geronimo Stilton Ruins Reenactment!

"Sales of *The Daily Rat* are going to go **UP, UP, UP**! And sales of *The Rodent's Gazette* are going to go down, down, down!"

Before we could stop her, Sally DASHED out of my cabin. We chased after her, but she was surprisingly fast! Once on deck, she dove headlong into the **SEA** and then boarded a waiting speedboat.

"You're finished, Stilton!" she yelled as she zoomed away. "YOUR CHEDDAR IS SHREDDED!"

SAY CHEESE!

Now that we knew Sally had been the saboteur, I felt **miserable**. Not only was it my fault the success of the reenactment had been put in danger, now Sally was going to publish embarrassing pictures of me!

I began to sob. "When Sally prints those photos, all of New Mouse City will be laughing at me!"

BERNARDO Almouse grinned. "**CALM DOWN**, Admiral. That cheesebrain won't be printing anything — because I have her photos!" he said triumphantly. "I took her CAMERA out of her bag while she was talking. Hee, hee, hee!"

I was so relieved, I gave Bernardo a giant hug! I thanked him from

SALLY RATMOUSEN'S PHOTOS

PHOTO #1
Geronimo was always seasick!

PHOTO #2
Geronimo's so clumsy, he kept falling in the water!

PHOTO #3
He had to be constantly rescued!

PHOTO #4
The seagulls even thought he was a fish!

the bottom of my heart and took a peek at Sally's photos.

Holey cheese! They were DREADFUL!

"You're a true friend," I said to Bernardo. "Thank you so much. I don't know what would have happened without you!"

"You would have been the laughingstock of NEW MOUSE CITY!" Trap said, snickering.

I smiled. "For once, Trap, you're right!" I agreed. I turned around to face the crew, who

Hooray!

We found the saboteur!

had gathered behind us. "Dear friends, all's well. We found the saboteur! To celebrate, we'll have a great big party. Paulina will COOK all her secret recipes!"

Everyone was THRILLED that the troublemaker had been unmasked. "Three cheers for Admiral Stilton! Hooray! Hooray! Hooray!"

In the moonlight a few hours later, we had a fabumouse banquet on the deck.

Hooray! Hooray! Hooray!

ANOTHER DA GAMA!

The following morning I woke up with a start. I heard a loud noise coming from above.

FLAP! FLAP! FLAP! FLAP! FLAP! FLAP! FLAP! FLAP! FLAP! FLAP! FLAP! FLAP! FLAP! FLAP! FLAP! FLA

FLAP! FLAP! FLAP! FLAP! FLAP! FLAP! FLAP! FLAP!

The noise was getting **LOUDER AND LOUDER**! What could it be? I quickly got dressed and ran out on deck. A *gusty wind* nearly knocked me head over paws. Double-twisted rat tails! It was a helicopter! A few seconds later, **Secretary Rattio**

climbed down from the helicopter. With him was a rodent I didn't recognize, wearing a **Vasco Da Gama** costume just like mine. As soon as they touched the ground, the secretary came over to me.

"Mr. Stilton, **I'm so sorry**, but we've made a terrible mistake. You're actually not a descendant of Vasco da Gama. The real descendant is this gentlemouse, **Victor da Gamouse**!"

Welcome aboard!

Nice to meet you!

Geronimo Stilton, publisher of *The Rodent's Gazette*

Victor da Gamouse, expert sea captain

I shook Victor's paw. "Welcome aboard! I can tell right away that you are da Gama's descendant — you look just like him. You're a real slice off the old cheese block!"

The secretary looked EMBARRASSED. "Our historians mixed up the two of you in their report. Mr. Stilton, you are really a descendant of Luís de Camões. He's famouse for having written *The Lusiads,* an epic poem which tells the story of Vasco da Gama's journey."

I couldn't believe my ears! "I'm the descendant of a fabumouse writer!" I said. "No need to apologize. I'm truly honored!"

Secretary Rattio cleared his throat. "Therefore, Mr. Stilton, I want to thank you for all you've done so far, especially for exposing the saboteur. But Victor will be taking over the rest of the sea voyage,"

Luís de Camões and *The Lusiads*

LUÍS DE CAMÕES
(Born in Lisbon c. 1524, died in Lisbon June 10, 1580)

Luís de Camões is considered Portugal's greatest poet. His most famous work is *The Lusiads*, an epic poem.

THE LUSIADS (1572)
The Lusiads is an epic poem in ten sections that celebrates the history of Portugal, blending reality and myth. The epic also tells the story of Vasco da Gama's voyages and other Portuguese travelers who traveled past the Cape of Good Hope and from there opened up a new route to India.

he said, twisting his paws anxiously.

"I'm thrilled!" I exclaimed, relieved. "I can now honestly say that I don't know a thing about ships, sails, or navigation — and I get terribly **seasick**!"

"In that case," Secretary Rattio said, "how would you feel about spending the rest of your time in Portugal holding a series of lectures on **Luís de Camões** and his epic poem *The Lusiads*?"

Thea, Trap, Bugsy Wugsy, and Benjamin answered for me, all shouting together. "We accept! *When do we leave?*"

"Right now, if you want!" the secretary responded. "We could set up a seminar tomorrow morning at the Belém tower."

We said good-bye to the crew and packed up all our things. Half an hour later, we took off in the helicopter. Destination: **Lisbon**!

THERE'S NO PLACE LIKE HOME!

A week later, once the lectures were finished, we reluctantly left **Portugal** and returned to Mouse Island. Although I was glad to be back, I missed the beautiful places we had seen and all the new **friends** we had met: Secretary Rattio, Bernardo Almouse, Paulina Pecorina, and all the crewmice.

It had been a wonderful trip!

With a little regret, I unpacked my suitcase. Inside, I found the **Vasco Da Gama costume** I had worn during the *São Gabriel*'s voyage! The secretary must have

snuck it into my luggage while we were saying our good-byes. I carried it up to the attic, where I keep the mementos of my many other **ADVENTURES**.

In the suitcase was also an old and valuable 𝔼𝔻𝕀𝕋𝕀𝕆ℕ of the works of **Luís de Camões**, my famouse ancestor. The books were given to me as a parting gift by the

So many memories!

secretary. I took them to my library and placed them carefully on the bookcase, right in front of my desk. There, they'd always be close to me, and would remind me of LISBON and the boat voyage — and of a special piece of my heritage!

I couldn't wait to see what other mementos my future journeys would bring. And I know I'll do my great ancestor proud by WRITING about every adventure! Until next time, dear mouse friends!

Be sure to read all my fabumouse adventures!

#1 Lost Treasure of the Emerald Eye   #2 The Curse of the Cheese Pyramid   #3 Cat and Mouse in a Haunted House   #4 I'm Too Fond of My Fur!   #5 Four Mice Deep in the Jungle

#6 Paws Off, Cheddarface!   #7 Red Pizzas for a Blue Count   #8 Attack of the Bandit Cats   #9 A Fabumouse Vacation for Geronimo   #10 All Because of a Cup of Coffee

#11 It's Halloween, You 'Fraidy Mouse!   #12 Merry Christmas, Geronimo!   #13 The Phantom of the Subway   #14 The Temple of the Ruby of Fire   #15 The Mona Mousa Code

#16 A Cheese-Colored Camper   #17 Watch Your Whiskers, Stilton!   #18 Shipwreck on the Pirate Islands   #19 My Name Is Stilton, Geronimo Stilton   #20 Surf's Up, Geronimo!

 #21 The Wild, Wild West

 #22 The Secret of Cacklefur Castle

 A Christmas Tale

 #23 Valentine's Day Disaster

 #24 Field Trip to Niagara Falls

 #25 The Search for Sunken Treasure

 #26 The Mummy with No Name

 #27 The Christmas Toy Factory

 #28 Wedding Crasher

 #29 Down and Out Down Under

 #30 The Mouse Island Marathon

 #31 The Mysterious Cheese Thief

 Christmas Catastrophe

 #32 Valley of the Giant Skeletons

 #33 Geronimo and the Gold Medal Mystery

 #34 Geronimo Stilton, Secret Agent

 #35 A Very Merry Christmas

 #36 Geronimo's Valentine

 #37 The Race Across America

 #38 A Fabumouse School Adventure

 #39 Singing Sensation

 #40 The Karate Mouse

 #41 Mighty Mount Kilimanjaro

 #42 The Peculiar Pumpkin Thief

 #43 I'm Not a Supermouse!

#44 The Giant
Diamond Robbery

#45 Save the White
Whale!

#46 The Haunted
Castle

#47 Run for the Hills,
Geronimo!

#48 The Mystery in
Venice

#49 The Way of
the Samurai

#50 This Hotel Is
Haunted!

#51 The Enormouse
Pearl Heist

#52 Mouse in Space!

#53 Rumble in
the Jungle

#54 Get into Gear,
Stilton!

#55 The Golden
Statue Plot

#56 Flight of the
Red Bandit

Special Edition!
The Hunt for the
Golden Book

#57 The Stinky
Cheese Vacation

#58 The Super
Chef Contest

#59 Welcome to
Moldy Manor

Special Edition!
The Hunt for the
Curious Cheese

#60 The Treasure of
Easter Island

#61 Mouse House
Hunter

#62 Mouse
Overboard!

Up Next!

Special Edition!
The Hunt for the
Secret Papyrus

Join me and my friends as we travel through time in these very special editions!

THE JOURNEY THROUGH TIME

BACK IN TIME:
THE SECOND JOURNEY THROUGH TIME

THE RACE AGAINST TIME:
THE THIRD JOURNEY THROUGH TIME

Don't miss any of these exciting Thea Sisters adventures!

Thea Stilton and the
Dragon's Code

Thea Stilton and the
Mountain of Fire

Thea Stilton and the
Ghost of the Shipwreck

Thea Stilton and the
Secret City

Thea Stilton and the
Mystery in Paris

Thea Stilton and the
Cherry Blossom Adventure

Thea Stilton and the
Star Castaways

Thea Stilton: Big Trouble
in the Big Apple

Thea Stilton and the
Ice Treasure

Thea Stilton and the
Secret of the Old Castle

Thea Stilton and the
Blue Scarab Hunt

Thea Stilton and the
Prince's Emerald

Thea Stilton and the Mystery
on the Orient Express

Thea Stilton and the
Dancing Shadows

Thea Stilton and the
Legend of the Fire Flowers

Thea Stilton and the
Spanish Dance Mission

Thea Stilton and the
Journey to the Lion's Den

Thea Stilton and the
Great Tulip Heist

Thea Stilton and the
Chocolate Sabotage

Thea Stilton and the
Missing Myth

Thea Stilton and the
Lost Letters

Thea Stilton and the
Tropical Treasure

Thea Stilton and the
Hollywood Hoax

Be sure to read all of our magical special edition adventures!

THE KINGDOM OF FANTASY

THE QUEST FOR PARADISE:
THE RETURN TO THE KINGDOM OF FANTASY

THE AMAZING VOYAGE:
THE THIRD ADVENTURE IN THE KINGDOM OF FANTASY

THE DRAGON PROPHECY:
THE FOURTH ADVENTURE IN THE KINGDOM OF FANTASY

THE VOLCANO OF FIRE:
THE FIFTH ADVENTURE IN THE KINGDOM OF FANTASY

THE SEARCH FOR TREASURE:
THE SIXTH ADVENTURE IN THE KINGDOM OF FANTASY

THE ENCHANTED CHARMS:
THE SEVENTH ADVENTURE IN THE KINGDOM OF FANTASY

THE PHOENIX OF DESTINY:
AN EPIC KINGDOM OF FANTASY ADVENTURE

THE HOUR OF MAGIC:
THE EIGHTH ADVENTURE IN THE KINGDOM OF FANTASY

THEA STILTON: THE JOURNEY TO ATLANTIS

THEA STILTON: THE SECRET OF THE FAIRIES

THEA STILTON: THE SECRET OF THE SNOW

THEA STILTON: THE CLOUD CASTLE

MEET GERONIMO STILTONIX

He is a spacemouse — the Geronimo Stilton of a parallel universe! He is captain of the spaceship *MouseStar 1*. While flying through the cosmos, he visits distant planets and meets crazy aliens. His adventures are out of this world!

#1 Alien Escape

#2 You're Mine, Captain!

#3 Ice Planet Adventure

#4 The Galactic Goal

#5 Rescue Rebellion

#6 The Underwater Planet

#7 Beware! Space Junk!

Meet
GERONIMO STILTONOOT

He is a cavemouse — Geronimo Stilton's ancient ancestor! He runs the stone newspaper in the prehistoric village of Old Mouse City. From dealing with dinosaurs to dodging meteorites, his life in the Stone Age is full of adventure!

#1 The Stone of Fire

#2 Watch Your Tail!

#3 Help, I'm in Hot Lava!

#4 The Fast and the Frozen

#5 The Great Mouse Race

#6 Don't Wake the Dinosaur!

#7 I'm a Scaredy-Mouse!

#8 Surfing for Secrets

#9 Get the Scoop, Geronimo!

#10 My Autosaurus Will Win!

#11 Sea Monster Surprise

ABOUT THE AUTHOR

 Born in New Mouse City, Mouse Island, **GERONIMO STILTON** is Rattus Emeritus of Mousomorphic Literature and of Neo-Ratonic Comparative Philosophy. For the past twenty years, he has been running *The Rodent's Gazette,* New Mouse City's most widely read daily newspaper.

Stilton was awarded the Ratitzer Prize for his scoops on *The Curse of the Cheese Pyramid* and *The Search for Sunken Treasure.* He has also received the Andersen 2000 Prize for Personality of the Year. One of his bestsellers won the 2002 eBook Award for world's best ratlings' electronic book. His works have been published all over the globe.

In his spare time, Mr. Stilton collects antique cheese rinds and plays golf. But what he most enjoys is telling stories to his nephew Benjamin.

1. Main entrance
2. Printing presses (where the books and newspaper are printed)
3. Accounts department
4. Editorial room (where the editors, illustrators, and designers work)
5. Geronimo Stilton's office
6. Helicopter landing pad

THE RODENT'S GAZETTE

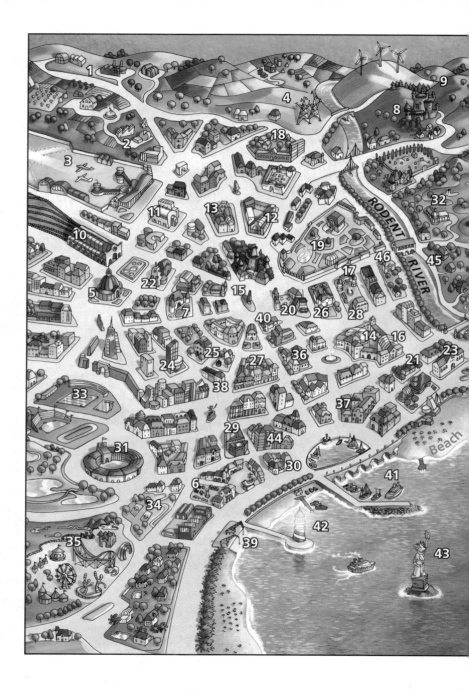

Map of New Mouse City

1. Industrial Zone
2. Cheese Factories
3. Angorat International Airport
4. WRAT Radio and Television Station
5. Cheese Market
6. Fish Market
7. Town Hall
8. Snotnose Castle
9. The Seven Hills of Mouse Island
10. Mouse Central Station
11. Trade Center
12. Movie Theater
13. Gym
14. Catnegie Hall
15. Singing Stone Plaza
16. The Gouda Theater
17. Grand Hotel
18. Mouse General Hospital
19. Botanical Gardens
20. Cheap Junk for Less (Trap's store)
21. Aunt Sweetfur and Benjamin's House
22. Mouseum of Modern Art
23. University and Library
24. *The Daily Rat*
25. *The Rodent's Gazette*
26. Trap's House
27. Fashion District
28. The Mouse House Restaurant
29. Environmental Protection Center
30. Harbor Office
31. Mousidon Square Garden
32. Golf Course
33. Swimming Pool
34. Tennis Courts
35. Curlyfur Island Amusement Park
36. Geronimo's House
37. Historic District
38. Public Library
39. Shipyard
40. Thea's House
41. New Mouse Harbor
42. Luna Lighthouse
43. The Statue of Liberty
44. Hercule Poirat's Office
45. Petunia Pretty Paws's House
46. Grandfather William's House

Map of Mouse Island

Dear mouse friends,
Thanks for reading, and farewell
till the next book.
It'll be another whisker-licking-good
adventure, and that's a promise!

Geronimo Stilton